Bob the Builder™

Dizzy Mix-up

Bob was having an early morning cup of tea before he started work.

"Miaow!" cried Pilchard, who wanted to play.

"Sorry, Pilchard. I've got lots to do. I'll play later," Bob promised.

Wendy and all the machines were waiting for Bob in the yard.

"Today we're going to put bollards around the town hall," Bob told them.

Dizzy looked puzzled. "Ooh, what are bollards?"

"They're things you stick in the ground to stop the traffic," Bob explained.

"Mrs Potts is having some garden statues delivered," Wendy told Bob. "She was hoping you could dig a few holes before they arrived."

"A few holes shouldn't take too long," said Bob.

"Thanks, Bob," said Wendy. "Mrs Potts will be very relieved."

Bob loaded the road drill into Muck's front scoop, then put edging stones into Scoop's shovel.

"What can I take, Bob?" squeaked Dizzy.

"How about a big bag of cement?" chuckled Bob.

They were soon all loaded up and ready to go.

"See you later," rumbled Roley.

"Yeah… er, bye!" said Lofty, a little nervously.

"**Can we dig it?**" called Bob as they clattered out of the yard.

"**Yes we can!**" cried Muck, Scoop and Dizzy.

When they arrived at the town hall Bob showed Dizzy and Muck where to start work. Then he set off on Scoop to Mrs Potts' house.

Bob found Mrs Potts in her garden.

"Morning, Mrs Potts," he called. "Now, how many holes do you want me to dig?"

"Well, I've got my frog statue here, that's one," said Mrs Potts.

"He doesn't look very happy!" joked Bob.

"There are also two dancing fairies, a pixie, a goblin, a windmill... and something else that I just can't remember... "

"Right then, I'll dig a few holes to start with," said Bob.

When Bob had finished, he and Scoop left for the town hall to meet Dizzy and Muck.

First, Bob drew a line of chalk crosses on the road in front of the town hall. Then he lifted the heavy road drill out of Muck's front scoop.

"Cover your ears!" he yelled to the machines, as he put on his ear protectors and safety goggles. "This is going to be really **LOUD!**"

Bob switched on the drill and held on tight. It screeched and started to shatter the hard concrete. Vibrations from the powerful drill made Dizzy bounce wildly up and down!

Finally the holes were dug, and Bob turned off the road drill.

"Now, Scoop," he said. "Let's have those edging stones."

Bob lifted the big stones out of Scoop's front shovel and put them down.

"Oh, no. They're too big!" he cried. "We'll have to go back to the yard and get the right ones," he told Scoop.

"No prob, Bob!" Scoop replied cheerfully.

Bob told Dizzy and Muck to wait outside the town hall, just in case the delivery man turned up with the bollards.

"Bye!" called Muck and Dizzy as Bob and Scoop rumbled off.

Back at the yard, Wendy was on the phone to Mrs Potts, who was worried because her statues hadn't been delivered.

"I have to go out to the shops," she flustered.

"Don't worry," soothed Wendy. "I'm sure your statues won't arrive while you're out."

Wendy smiled as she put down the phone. "Dear Mrs Potts. She's always worrying about something!"

Muck and Dizzy were also waiting for a delivery. They were very surprised when a lorry load of garden statues was left on the pavement in front of the town hall. Two dancing fairies, a pixie, a goblin, a windmill and a Greek god!

"Hee, hee, hee! That pixie looks like Lofty in a bad mood!" giggled Dizzy.

Muck laughed at one of the statues that was waving its arms in the air.

"This fairy looks just like Spud scaring away the birds!"

Suddenly Dizzy had one of her great ideas.

"Muck! Why don't we surprise Bob and put the statues up for him?"

"Yeah!" replied an excited Muck.

Dizzy quickly mixed up some concrete and poured it into the holes, then Muck pushed the statues into place with his front shovel.

"Up a bit… to me a bit!" Dizzy directed.

Muck staggered under the weight of the heavy goblin.

"Put it **there!**" cried Dizzy.

"**Pheww!**" Muck sighed with relief as he plonked the statue down.

Dizzy and Muck looked very pleased with themselves as they stared at the statues.

One of the fairies was upside down, the windmill was stuck in sideways, the goblin had gone in head-first and the Greek god had fallen over!

"**Wow!** We're really good at this," said Muck.

Dizzy jumped up and down with excitement.

"Muck!" she squeaked. "Why don't we go and help Mrs Potts next?"

"Yeah," Muck agreed. "It'll be another big surprise for Bob!"

At Mrs Potts' house, they found a pile of bollards neatly stacked by the back door.

"Look, Muck," said Dizzy. "Mrs Potts has left everything out for us."

"What does she want bollards for?" puzzled Muck.

"Maybe she thinks they're pretty!" giggled Dizzy.

"Pretty ugly!" sniggered Muck.

Dizzy carefully poured concrete into the holes that Bob had dug in Mrs Potts' garden. Muck picked up the bollards and dropped them in one by one.
Plop! Plop! Plop!

Meanwhile, Bob and Scoop were outside the town hall, staring in horror at Mrs Potts' statues.

"I don't believe it!" gasped Bob.

"Bob, if the statues are **here**," Scoop spluttered, waving his scoop, "**Where** are the bollards?"

Bob went very pale and put his hands to his head.

"Oh, Scoop," he gulped. "You don't think...?"

Scoop's pistons popped as he asked the big question: "Where are Dizzy and Muck?"

"**Oh, no! Not Mrs Potts' garden!**" yelled Bob.

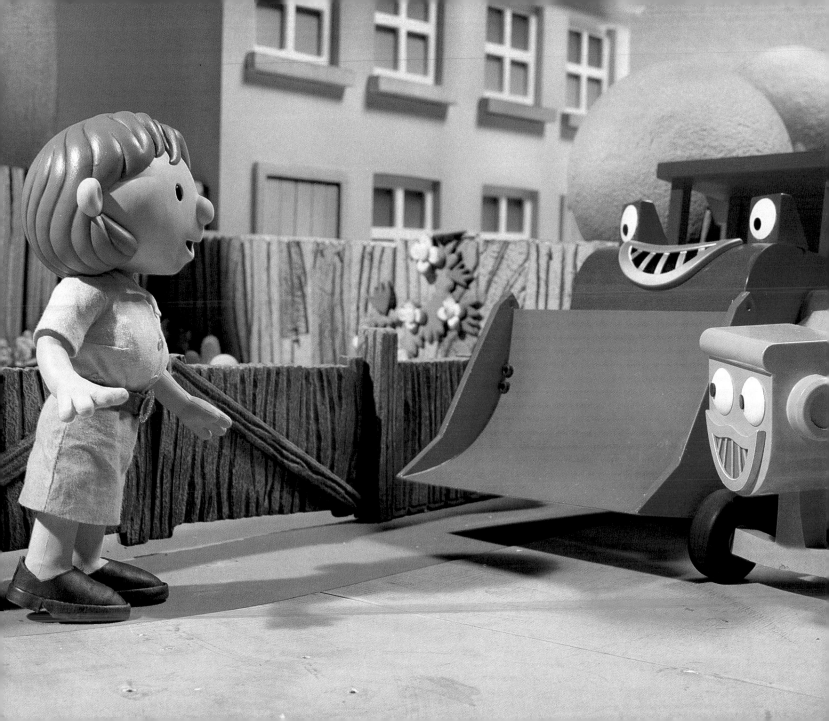

When Mrs Potts came back from the shops and saw the bollards stuck outside her front door, she stared in amazement.

"Where are my garden statues?" gasped Mrs Potts.

"Do you like them?" Dizzy asked proudly.

"What's going on?" Mrs Potts asked.

Dizzy and Muck looked at each other.

"Your statues?" asked Muck.

"Er, well, er, we thought… er…" dithered Dizzy as she realised what they'd done.

Just then, Bob came roaring up, on Scoop.

"What have they done?" Mrs Potts asked.

Bob stared at Dizzy and Muck, and then at Mrs Potts' front garden.

"Oh, dear!" he groaned.

"We were only trying to help!" cried Muck.
"R-e-a-l-l-y we were," Dizzy insisted.
"But... where are my statues?" wondered Mrs Potts.
"Don't worry," Bob assured her. "I know exactly
where your statues are."

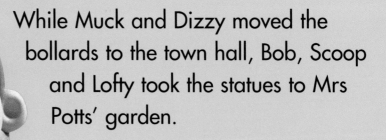

While Muck and Dizzy moved the
bollards to the town hall, Bob, Scoop
and Lofty took the statues to Mrs
Potts' garden.

"Er… what shall I do with this, Bob?" asked Lofty, as he dangled the Greek god from his hook.

"Put it right here," said Bob, carefully lowering the statue into a hole in the garden.

"My Greek god!" cried Mrs Potts in delight. "That's the one I couldn't remember."

At last, all the statues were safely stuck in their holes.

"Oh! Aren't they beautiful?" Mrs Potts beamed.

"Er… they're very nice," Bob muttered politely.

Mrs Potts picked up her frog statue.

"Oh dear, what about him?" asked Bob.

"He's a little present for you!" laughed Mrs Potts as she pushed the frog into Bob's hands.

Bob stared at the frog and started to laugh. "Thank you, Mrs Potts. He's just what I always wanted!"

THE END!